TINKLE
WHERE LEARNING MEETS FUN

SHIKARI SHAMBU'S ESCAPADES!

Log on to: www.tinkleonline.com

SHIKARI SHAMBU

The Looting Langur

Based on a story sent by :
Srinivas T.R.

Illustrations : Savio Mascarenhas

MRS SHAMBU WAS PACKING TO GO TO HER SISTER'S HOUSE.

MY SISTER IS GOING TO LOVE THIS NAPKIN I EMBROIDERED FOR HER. I'LL GIVE IT TO HER ALONG WITH THESE ORANGES.

I MUST COOK AND FREEZE SOME FOOD FOR THAT LAZY SHAMBU.

JUST THEN—

TRA LA LA...

...AHA! A NAPKIN. JUST WHAT I NEED TO WIPE A SWEATY FACE WITH.

NOW I WILL GO FOR A LONG WALK IN THE WOODS WITH THESE ORANGES FOR A WAYSIDE SNACK.

NOT TOO FAR AWAY—

SCREECH!

CHASE THAT LANGUR AWAY. HE HAS STRIPPED THE GUAVA TREE OF EVERY GUAVA.

YECH!

YARGH!

SPLAT!

SPLOTCH!

2

THIS LANGUR MUST BE TAUGHT A LESSON.

LET'S TELL SHIKARI SHAMBU.

MEANWHILE —

EEEK! WHERE ARE THE GIFTS FOR MY SISTER?

MUDDY FOOTPRINTS! IT HAS TO BE SHAMBU. HE HAS TAKEN THE BASKET OF ORANGES TOO!

JUST WAIT...

... TILL I ...

... CATCH HIM!

IN A NEARBY VILLAGE —

AIYEEEE! THAT WICKED LANGUR HAS TAKEN MY CLOTHES.

HE UPTURNED MY BOTTLE OF OIL.

3

THE LANGUR WAS HAVING A WONDERFUL TIME.

HUMANS ARE SO EASY TO TEASE. WHEN THEY ARE ANGRY THEY LOOK SO FUNNY.

A LITTLE LATER —

TRA LA LA LA LAAAA...

EEYOOO! WHAT A TERRIBLE SOUND.

IT WAS SHIKARI SHAMBU.

COOL GRASS, TINKLING STREAM AND NO SHANTI. JUST THE PLACE TO EAT ORANGES.

BUT —

CHATTER

SWIPE

YAARGH! A GREEDY LANGUR!

.. THOSE ORANGES ARE MINE.

AS SHAMBU RAN —

SWISH

4

SPLAT

THUNK

A LITTLE LATER —

GOT HIM! SNOOZING LIKE A BABY. HE THINKS THAT THE DISGUISE WILL FOOL ME.

GIVE ME MY NAPKIN AND ORANGES, YOU ....

BONK

OH NO! THIS IS NOT SHAMBU, IT IS A LANGUR.

WHY IS IT SO DARK?

JUST THEN —

SHANTI!

SHIKARI SHAMBU! YOU'VE TAUGHT THE NASTY LANGUR A LESSON.

THE LANGUR DECIDED HE HAD HAD ENOUGH.

I WILL MOVE TO SOME OTHER JUNGLE. THIS PLACE IS NOT FOR ME.

THREE CHEERS FOR SHAMBU. HMPH!

SHIKARI SHAMBU
TWO MONKEYS AND A MUFFLER

Story by: Aashish Jindal
Script: Aditi Jayakar

Illustrations: Savio Mascarenhas

IT WAS A COLD DAY IN OCTOBER AND SHAMBU WAS AT HOME.

BRR... SHANTI, I'M FREEZING. I WISH I WERE A SHEEP WITH A COAT OF WOOL !

HERE'S SOME COFFEE, YOU WILL FEEL BETTER.

JUST AS SHAMBU WAS GETTING COMFORTABLE —

SHAMBUJI, SHAMBUJI, ARE YOU HOME ?

OH NO ! NOT NOW ! SHANTI, PLEASE TELL THEM I'M OUT. PLEASE !

DON'T BE LAZY, SHAMBU.

SHANTI OPENED THE DOOR AND LED THE VISITOR IN.

HELLO, SHAMBUJI, I'M BHOLA. THIS IS TOPI, A MONKEY WHO ESCAPED FROM THE ZOO. PLEASE KEEP HIM WITH YOU TILL THE ZOO AUTHORITIES ARRIVE.

I'M GETTING READY, SHAMBU. WE HAVE TO GO TO MY MOTHER'S HOUSE FOR LUNCH.

HEY, TOPI! WHAT ARE YOU DOING?

HE'S THROWING IT BACK TO YOU. HOW SWEET! HE WANTS TO PLAY WITH YOU. I'LL BE READY IN FIFTEEN MINUTES, SHAMBU.

OKAY, SHANTI.

WHILE SHANTI WAS GONE —

GOOD THROW, TOPI! CHECK OUT THIS THROW!

CHEE CHEE CHEE!

I'M READY. OFF WE GO, SHAMBU! AND DON'T FORGET THE WAY THIS TIME.

COME ON TOPI!

DOESN'T SHE KNOW I DO IT ON PURPOSE? HEE HEE!

THEY DROVE FOR A LONG TIME THROUGH A THICK JUNGLE.

THE JUNGLE PATH LOOKS SO DIFFERENT IN THIS SEASON.

DON'T WORRY, I KNOW WHERE I AM GOING.

BUT—

AAAH! HELP!

AAAH!

AND—

CRASH

7

OH NO! OUR JEEP IS STUCK. WE'LL HAVE TO WALK A BIT. COME ON, SHANTI.

OOF! AGAIN THE WRONG HOOGAWAY. WHERE'S TOPI AND BOOGA! WHATS THAT SOUND?

HOOGA BOOGA!

HOOGA BOOGA!

WITHIN MINUTES —

HOOGA BOOGA!

HOOGA BOOGA!

HOOGA BOOGA!

HOOGA BOOGA!

HOOGA BOOGA!

HOOGA BOOGA!

HOOGA BOOGA!

HOOGA BOOGA!

YOU HAVE SEEN THE HOOGA BOOGA TRIBES SECRET TERRITORY! HOW DID YOU DARE! MEN, OFF WITH THEIR HEADS!

OOOH, SHAMBU!

OOOH SHANTI!

BUT SHAMBU HAD TO BE BRAVE, SO —

DEAR MR HOOGA BOOGA, ISN'T THERE ANYWAY WE CAN BE SET FREE?

NEVER NO ONE EVER ESCAPES UNLESS THEY DO SOME HOOGA BOOGA!

8

HOOGA BOOGA? WHAT'S THAT?

MAGIC, MYSTERIOUS MAGIC. ONLY THEN CAN YOU GO, FOR THOSE WITH A PURE HEART HAVE MAGIC!

OH! THAT'S EASY. I CAN WALK WITH MY HAT OVER MY EYES.

JUST THEN, TO SHAMBU'S DELIGHT A BUSH RUSTLED —

?

TOPI! I HAVE AN IDEA.

RUSTLE

O CHIEF! I CAN MAKE THIS MUFFLER, THIS MAGIC MUFFLER COME TO LIFE.

HEH?

SHAMBU FLIPPED HIS MUFFLER INTO THE BUSH...

...AND THE MUFFLER CAME BACK.

THIS WENT ON...

...TILL—

STOP! STOP! YOU HAVE A PURE HEART! YOU CAN DO MAGIC! WE SHALL HELP YOU OUT OF HERE! FORGIVE ME! FORGIVE ME!

WONDERFUL! HOW DID YOU MANAGE THAT, SHAMBU? AND HEY! WHERE'S YOUR MUFFLER?

LOOK BEHIND YOU! HEE HEE!

SHIKARI SHAMBU

Fox Hunt

Based on a story sent by : Naveen M.

Illustrations : Savio Mascarenhas

SHIKARI SHAMBU HAD A GUEST.

SHAMBU, MY PRECIOUS SON-IN-LAW!

S 10

GOOD TO SEE YOU AGAIN, MOTHER-IN-LAW.

SHANTI'S MOTHER WAS PAYING A VISIT.

SHE WAS VERY FOND OF SHAMBU.

MOTHER, WHAT ARE YOU DOING?

FRYING PANCAKES FOR MY SON-IN-LAW.

MOTHER, WHAT ARE YOU KNITTING?

WOOLLEN SOCKS FOR MY SON-IN-LAW.

WHAT A BIG FUSS! HMPH!! SHE NEVER LIKED HIM AT FIRST. NOW SHE DOTES ON HIM.

ONE DAY —

SHAMBU, THIS IS JUNG LEE, CHIEF FOREST OFFICER. THREE FOXES HAVE WANDERED OUT OF THE SANCTUARY. ONE OF THEM IS GOING TO HAVE CUBS.

FOXES.. THAT'LL BE EASY. I'LL LOOK FOR THEM.

AND SO —

YOO HOO, SON-IN-LAW! CAN I HOP IN TOO?

SURE.

GRRRR.. THAT LEAVES ME TO COOK AND CLEAN ON MY OWN.

NOT FAR AWAY —

HA! I CAN GET OUT OF THIS DISGUISE NOW.

IT WAS KALLU, THE POACHER. HE HAD ESCAPED FROM PRISON.

MY FIRST JOB IS TO GET THAT WRETCHED SHIKARI SHAMBU. HE IS THE ONE WHO HAD ME LOCKED UP!

MEANWHILE —

WHAT A BEAUTIFUL PLACE, SON-IN-LAW! CAN WE STOP HERE FOR A WHILE?

OF COURSE. I WILL LOOK AROUND FOR THE FOXES.

AS SHAMBU TIPTOED THROUGH THE FOREST —

WHERE COULD THEY BE?

WHAT LUCK! THE MAN HIMSELF! HE HAS WALKED TO HIS DOOM. I WILL GET HIM NOW.

BUT IT WAS NOT EASY.

WHAT IS HE DOING?

11

MMF!

PHTOOEY!

THEY ARE SOMEWHERE CLOSE BY.

ACTUALLY, THE THREE FOXES WERE CLOSER TO SHAMBU'S MOTHER-IN-LAW.

LOOK AT THAT FUNNY LADY.

SHE LOOKS KIND.

MAYBE SHE'LL HAVE SOMETHING TO EAT.

AND SO —

YAP YAP

EH!?

YAP YAP YAP YAP

SHAMBU'S MOTHER-IN-LAW GOT THE FRIGHT OF HER LIFE...

EEEEEEEE!

...AND SO DID THE FOXES.

EEEEEEE

YELP!

YELP!

YELP!

12

MEANWHILE —

AH! I HAVE HIM, FINALLY.

PREPARE TO MEET YOUR DOOM.

HUH!?

BUT IT WAS KALLU'S BAD DAY.

EEEEEEEEEEEEEEEEEE

!?

A FIGURE WHIZZED TOWARDS THEM...

EEEEEEEEE

...AND —

CRASH

MUCH LATER —

WAS THAT A TRUCK.. A TANK..OR THE TITANIC?

HE HAS LOST HIS SENSES.

AND THEN SHAMBU GOT A CALL ON HIS MOBILE PHONE.

THE FOXES HAVE COME BACK ON THEIR OWN, SHAMBU. THEY SEEM TO HAVE GOT A NASTY SCARE.

HMM..I WONDER WHAT THEY SAW.

WE KNOW, DON'T WE!?

SHIKARI SHAMBU

Easy Catch

Readers' Choice

Based on a story sent by:
Vijay,

Illustrations:
Savio Mascarenhas

SHAMBU YOU ARE ALWAYS SLEEPING.. BLAH.. BLAH.. YADA.. YADA.. BLAH.. BLAH.

ZZZZ ZZZZ

LET ME TICKLE HIM WITH MY DUSTER. THAT WILL WAKE HIM UP.

JUST THEN —

DING DONG

SIGH!

IS SHIKARI SHAMBU HOME? WE WANT HIM TO CAPTURE A MANEATER FOR US.

YOU HAVE TO COME WITH US, SHAMBUJI, A MAN-EATER IS TROUBLING US.

SOON—

WE HAVE REACHED THE EDGE OF THE FOREST.

SHAMBUJI, ONLY A BRAVE PERSON LIKE YOU CAN GO AHEAD. WE TURN BACK FROM HERE.

OKAY, SEE YOU LATER.

SIGH! SUCH PEACE...

CHIRP-CHIRP CHIRP-CHIRP

...IF ONLY THERE WERE NO DANGEROUS ANIMALS IN THE JUNGLE.

OUCH!

15

I'LL GET THIS HUMAN.

AND SO—

ROAR

EEEEE

PUFF! PUFF! PUFF! PUFF!

PHEW! THE TIGER CAN'T GET TO ME HERE. OOPS!

PLOP

!

HEY, WHAT'S THIS? WHY CAN'T I SEE?

THE TIGER CAN'T SEE. NOW IS MY CHANCE TO ESCAPE.

MEANWHILE, TWO POACHERS WERE ON THE LOOKOUT FOR A CATCH.

LOOK, THERE'S SHAMBU.

LET'S TEACH HIM A LESSON.

GOT THE SNEAKY SHIKARI!

LET ME QUICKLY MAKE A GET AWAY.

THWACK

HA! HA! WE'VE FINALLY GOT RID OF HIM.

BUT AT THAT MOMENT SHAMBU PEERED THROUGH THE GRASS.

AAAAH! IT'S SHAMBU...

...IT'S HIS GHOST.

I THINK I'LL GO HOME AND COME BACK LATER TO GET MY HAT.

SOME FOREST OFFICIALS WERE ON THE ROUNDS OF THE FOREST.

LOOK, SHAMBU HAS DONE IT. HE'S CAUGHT THE MANEATER.

AND HE LEFT HIS HAT TO TELL US THAT IT IS HIS HANDIWORK.

SHIKARI SHAMBU

SAMBOO SHAKES A TAIL

Based on a story sent by :
Bharath S.

Illustrations : Savio Mascarenhas

MRS SHAMBU WAS IN A VERY HAPPY MOOD.

DON'T YOU JUST LOVE MY NEPHEW, CHIMPOO.

NO, I DON'T. I HATE THE WAY HE CALLS ME....

UNCLE SAMBOO!

CHIMPOO WAS STUDYING IN THE U.S.A. AND HAD COME FOR A HOLIDAY TO INDIA.

SHAMBU. THE NAME IS SHAMBU.

NEVER MIND. SHOW HIM YOUR HUNTING TROPHIES.

SO —

I GOT THIS WHEN I CAPTURED A RHINO IN ASSAM.

!?

THIS TROPHY WAS GIVEN TO ME FOR KNOCKING OUT A POLAR BEAR IN GREENLAND.

NAAAA... NOT POSSIBLE.

WHAT DID YOU SAY?

THIS STUFF DOESN'T SEEM REAL, UNC.

I'LL SHOW YOU...

...YOU COME WITH ME.

WHERE ARE YOU GOING?

TO CATCH A LION.

?

SHIKARI SHAMBU HUNTED HIGH AND LOW FOR A LION...

...BUT LIONS ARE NOT EASY TO COME BY THESE DAYS.

MEOWR

YOW!

19

MEANWHILE AT THE DON BITTAKER SNAKE FARM —

POLONIUS IS GONE.

OH NO!

POLONIUS?

YES. HE IS MR BITTAKER'S PRIZED PYTHON.

POLONIUS WAS AN ADVENTUROUS YOUNG PYTHON.

LIVING IN A WELL IS NOT MY CUP OF TEA. I LIKE THE WILD OPEN SPACES.

THE DAY WORE ON.

NO LION... NO TIGER... NOT EVEN A PUNY PANTHER. WHAT'S HAPPENED TO ALL THE ANIMALS?

GIVE UP, UNC. LET'S GO HOME. YOU CAN SWAT FLIES INSTEAD.

YOU DON'T BELIEVE ME, HUH!? LET ME TELL YOU ABOUT THE TIME I FACED A MAN-EATING LEOPARD.

OOOOH!

I WAS STANDING BY A TREE EATING A SANDWICH WHEN I SAW SOMETHING DANGLING NEAR MY LEFT EYE.

?

A CLOSER LOOK REVEALED THAT IT WAS THE LEOPARD'S TAIL.

WATCH OUT, SHIKARI SHAMBU, THAT'S NOT A LEOPARD'S TAIL...

...IT IS POLONIUS, HAVING AN AFTERNOON NAP.

I CAUGHT THE WRETCH LIKE THIS...

ULP!

...PULLED IT DOWN...

...AND SWUNG IT ROUND AND ROUND OVER MY HEAD...

EEEP!

...TILL IT COLLAPSED.

YOU'VE C...C... CAUGHT A P...P... PYTHON, UNCLE SAMBOO.

I HAVE!?

JUST THEN—

SHIKARI SHAMBU, THANKS A MILLION FOR CATCHING POLONIUS.

HE CAME, HE SAW, HE CONQUERED. THAT'S MY UNCLE SAMBOO.

SHIKARI SHAMBU

AMNESIA TO THE RESCUE

Based on a story sent by :
Sumith Sivanand

Illustrations :
Savio Mascarenhas

SHAMBU WAS WALKING ALONG THINKING OF THE CIRCUS VISITING HIS TOWN. JUST THEN —

A WALLET ! I WONDER WHOSE IT IS.

MMM.. LET'S SEE IF THERE'S A NAME SOMEWHERE INSIDE IT...

... BANDINO — THE GREAT BANDINO ! SO, HE IS ALSO HERE FOR THE CIRCUS. I'LL GET TO MEET HIM WHEN I RETURN THIS TO HIM.

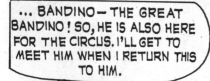

BANDINO WAS A FAMOUS ANIMAL TRAINER.

SUDDENLY —

TOING!

OUCH !

WHERE AM I ? OH ! OH ! MY HEAD IS HURTING.

JUST THEN——

SHAMBU SAHIB! SHAMBU SAHIB!

SHAMBU SAHIB? WHO'S THIS SHAMBU SAHIB?

SHAMBU HAS LOST HIS MEMORY! WILL HE MAKE A BETTER HUNTER NOW?

A RHINO HAS ESCAPED FROM THE CIRCUS AND IS CAUSING TERROR AMONG ALL OF US. ONLY YOU CAN CATCH IT, SHAMBU SAHIB.

HUH? NO ONE AROUND? IT'S ME THEY ARE TALKING TO.

YOU MUST HELP US, SHAMBU SAHIB.

YES, YES, OF COURSE.

SHAMBU WAS FEELING VERY BRAVE AND IMPORTANT.

A RHINO..HMM..FETCH A LASSO, I'LL SEE WHAT I CAN DO.

YES, AT ONCE.

ARMED WITH A LASSO, SHAMBU LED THE VILLAGERS UP THE FOREST PATH.

THERE IT IS, SAHIB.

WAIT TILL I CATCH IT!

?

23

THE RHINO KNEW THAT IT WAS BEATEN.

SIGH!

THUD!

HURRAY! SHAMBU HAS CONQUERED THE RHINO.

WHAT A MAN!

AS SHAMBU RODE TO THE CIRCUS IN TRIUMPH —

SHAMBU, COME HERE THIS INSTANT! YOU PROMISED TO TAKE ME SHOPPING.

IT WAS HIS WIFE, SHANTI.

HOW DARE HE IGNORE ME!

CLUNK!

THE HIT ON THE HEAD BROUGHT SHAMBU'S MEMORY BACK.

EH.. WHA.. WHERE AM I?

YOU WERE GREAT. YOU JUST NABBED THIS GREAT BIG RHINO.

I DI..I.. D!

SWOON

!

?

SHIKARI SHAMBU

BIKER BOY

Story:
L.R. Raja Baskar

Script:
Janaki Viswanathan

Illustrations:
Savio Mascarenhas

ONE AFTERNOON —

SHANTI, WHAT DO YOU THINK OF MY NEW MODE OF TRANSPORT?

A MOTORBIKE!!

VRRROOM

I'VE DECIDED TO CALL HER TUR-TUR. AND DON'T MISS MY HELMET.

BIKER BOY? OOH! LET'S GO ON A BIKE RIDE RIGHT NOW.

LET'S GO TO THE FUN FAIR NEAR THE MARKET.

TO THE FUN FAIR THEN, TUR-TUR.

WHAT SORT OF BIKER BOY ARE YOU, SHAMBU? YOU'RE SUPPOSED TO SPEED ALONG.

NO, NO. DRIVE SAFE, THAT'S MY MOTTO. RIGHT, TUR-TUR?

AT THE FAIR —

MELA

I'LL JUST PARK HER AND JOIN YOU.

ALL RIGHT.

26

SHAMBU SPENT QUITE SOME TIME PARKING HIS TUR-TUR.

HMMM... NOT HERE, IT'S TOO SUNNY.

NOT HERE EITHER. THOSE BOYS WILL HURT MY TUR-TUR. WHERE DO I PARK YOU?

HE FINALLY PARKED HIS TUR-TUR JUST NEXT TO THE GUTTER.

NOBODY WILL COME ANYWHERE NEAR YOU, MY DEAR.

CRAZY?

AND SHAMBU MADE HIS WAY TO THE FAIR, HAPPY AND AT PEACE.

BUT CAN THERE BE PEACE AND NO ANIMAL IN SIGHT WHEN SHAMBU IS AROUND? NO WAY!

SHAMBU, LOOK AT THAT ELEPHANT, ISN'T HE BEAUTIFUL?!

ULP! YES, YES.

HEY, YOU BIG FAT FELLOW!

WOULD YOU LIKE A NICE PAT?

OR A NICE WHACK!

STOP BOTHERING BUNTY, I SAY.

BUNTY?

THWACK

HA HA! BUNTY THE ELEPHANT!

SUCH A FUNNY NAME!

MY NAME IS FUNNY, EH?

27

SHAMBU LEAPT FORWARD WITH A BLOOD-CURDLING

TUR-TUR! DON'T TOUCH MY TUR-TUR!

TUR-TUR? WHAT'S THAT?

MUST BE HIS WAR CRY.

SHAMBU GOT TO HIS BELOVED TUR-TUR BEFORE BUNTY COULD.

DON'T WORRY, TUR-TUR, I'M HERE NOW.

OOPS, MY LEG IS SLIPPING!

AS BUNTY'S LEG SLIPPED —

AAH, I AM FALLING!

YEOW!

YECH!

WHAT A STINK!

THAT'S WHAT YOU DESERVE.

S P L A T

LATER WHEN BUNTY HAD CALMED DOWN AND WAS TAKEN AWAY —

YOU MUST NEVER TEASE AN ANIMAL OR HIT IT, BOYS.

SOB! WE WON'T.

EVER AGAIN!

THAT WAS CLEVER OF YOU, MR SHAMBU TO DIVERT THE ELEPHANT TO THE GUTTER.

I ESPECIALLY LIKED YOUR WAR CRY, TUR-TUR!

ER...HEH HEH!

SHIKARI SHAMBU

Catching Wolves

Based on a story sent by: Richa Singh.

Illustrations:
Savio Mascarenhas

SHIKARI SHAMBU WAS STROLLING THROUGH THE MARKET WITH SHANTI.

GO ON, SHANTI, GO AHEAD AND SHOP.

HUH? HOW CAN I SHOP WITHOUT ANY MONEY?

OH! HAVEN'T YOU HEARD OF WINDOW SHOPPING? JUST LOOK AND DON'T BUY! IT'S FUN, IT'S FREE, IT'S FANTASTIC.

IT'S FOOLISH AND FEATHER-BRAINED.

SUDDENLY SHE FROZE NEAR A JEWELLERY SHOP.

LOOK! AREN'T THOSE EARRINGS MARVELLOUS? ONLY 3000 RUPEES!

THEY ARE LOVELY TO LOOK AT, LOOK ALL YOU WANT.

SUDDENLY HIS EYE CAUGHT A POSTER ON THE WALL.

ANNUAL ANIMAL HUNT PRIZE RS 3000! CATCH THE WOLF AND WIN THE PRIZE. DATE JULY 7TH AT 10 A.M. JUNGLE LODGE.
MR LAKKAD RAM, THE FOREST CONSERVATOR HAS KINDLY AGREED TO DRESS UP AS THE WOLF.

SHANTI SAW IT TOO AND WAS THRILLED.

GO ON! TOMORROW IS 7TH JULY! BAG THE WOLF AND BUY ME MY EARRINGS!

NEXT MORNING —

YAWN! CAN I HAVE COFFEE AND BREAKFAST, SHANTI?

NO TIME FOR THAT. RISE AND SHINE! WE'LL EAT ON THE WAY.

SHAMBU WAS STILL SLEEPY.

ON THE WAY TO WHAT?

TO MY EARRINGS. I MEAN THE ANIMAL HUNT.

SO IT WAS THAT THE TWOSOME TUCKED INTO SANDWICHES WHILE DRIVING THE JEEP TO THE JUNGLE LODGE.

I LIKE PICNICS.

YOU'LL HAVE LOTS OF THEM IF YOU GET ME THE EARRINGS.

SUDDENLY THEY SAW A FOREST OFFICER WAVING WILDLY AT THEM.

SHIKARI SHAMBU! STOP! PLEASE STOP!

HEY! I'M GETTING LATE FOR THE CONTEST.

THE OFFICER LOOKED TROUBLED.

A WILD WOLF HAS ESCAPED FROM THE SANCTUARY. HE'S FIERCE AND DANGEROUS. ONLY YOU CAN HELP US, SHIKARI SHAMBU.

OKAY! TELL ME ABOUT IT TONIGHT! RIGHT NOW I'M BUSY.

THEY REACHED THE VENUE WHERE A LARGE CROWD HAD GATHERED.

THIS IS A TREASURE HUNT WHERE YOU HAVE TO LOOK FOR A MAN DISGUISED AS A WOLF. THE PERSON WHO CATCHES HIM WILL WIN 3000 RUPEES.

HEY! THERE'S MY ARCH ENEMY, SHIKARI SHAMBU.

IT WAS SHAMBU'S OLD ENEMY J.J.

J.J. WANTED TO WIN THE CONTEST AND ALSO HARASS SHIKARI SHAMBU.

BUT ONCE SHAMBU WAS OUT OF SHANTI'S SIGHT HE TOOK IT EASY.

HMM! I'LL SIT UNDER THIS TREE AND TAKE A NAP.

SOON HE DOZED OFF.

THERE HE IS! I'LL KEEP AN EYE ON HIM FROM HERE.

ZZZZ

MEANWHILE THE WOLF FROM THE ZOO REACHED THE JUNGLE TOO...

...AND MET MR LAKKAD RAM IN WOLF'S CLOTHING.

MR LAKKAD RAM FAINTED...

...AND SHAMBU WOKE.

32

SHAMBU COULD NOT BELIEVE HIS LUCK.

HMM? HOW DID I GET SO LUCKY? THE FANCY DRESS WOLF IS RIGHT BEFORE MY EYES.

AND MISTAKING THE WOLF FOR THE MAN IN DISGUISE HE DRAGGED THE WOLF BEHIND HIM.

COME ALONG, MY PRETTY PRIZE!

!?

J.J. SAW THE SCENE AND WAS THRILLED.

HE GRABBED A BIG ROCK IN HIS HAND.

I WILL KILL TWO BIRDS WITH ONE STONE. I WILL KNOCK OUT SHAMBU AND TAKE THE WOLF. TEE HEE HEE.

YOU CAN GROWL LIKE A REAL WOLF!

GRRA

J.J. AIMED CAREFULLY AT SHAMBU'S HEAD. BUT—

THE WOLF WAS KNOCKED OUT.

HERE IS YOUR WOLF!

IT'S THE REAL WOLF!

MEANWHILE MR LAKKAD RAM RECOVERED.

THERE'S A REAL WOLF HERE! TAKE CARE.

WHY SHOULD WE FEAR WHEN SHIKARI SHAMBU IS HERE!

SHIKARI SHAMBU WON THE CONTEST AS WELL AS A REWARD FROM THE ZOO.

SHIKHARI SHAMBU
BEAR GOES BANANAS

Based on a story sent by: **Mujahid Chowdhury,**

Illustrations: Savio Mascarenhas

LATE ONE AFTERNOON IN THE SHAMBU HOUSEHOLD—

IT IS STRANGE...

ZZZZZZZ.

...AND MOST UNUSUAL THAT WHILE SHANTI SLEEPS PEACEFULLY...

...I HAVE BEEN WIDE AWAKE FOR THREE HOURS!

AIEEEEEE!

CAN'T A PERSON SLEEP IN PEACE?

SIGH... THAT USED TO BE MY FAVOURITE LINE.

I AM GOING OUT NOW. MAYBE I WILL FEEL SLEEPY WHEN I GET BACK.

UH...HUH? ZZZZ.

POOR SHAMBU WALKED ABOUT AIMLESSLY IN THE MARKET.

WHAT'S THAT NEW SHOP? LET ME GO IN AND CHECK.

SWEETY SNACKS

THE SLEEP SHOP

AH, IT'S THE FAMOUS MR SHAMBU HIMSELF. WHAT WOULD YOU LIKE TO SEE?

I HAVE NOT BEEN ABLE TO SLEEP....

SAY NO MORE, MR SHAMBU. I HAVE JUST THE THING FOR YOU. THE HAMMOCK, PERFECT FOR ANY SORT OF SLEEP. CATNAPS, FORTY WINKS OR A NICE LONG SLUMBER. JUST LIE IN, POP A COMPLIMENTARY BANANA AND SLEEP WILL NEVER LEAVE YOU.

SOUNDS LIKE A DREAM!

BUNCH OF BANANAS FREE

I WILL TAKE A HAMMOCK.

WONDERFUL! AND YOU GET A FREE BUNCH OF BANANAS.

AS SHAMBU CAME OUT OF THE SHOP —

I'LL COME BACK IF IT DOESN'T WORK.

OF COURSE IT WILL!

EACH BANANA HAS A SLEEPING PILL IN IT, YOU SILLY SHIKARI.

MEANWHILE BACK HOME —

HELLO, MR RATAN? SHAMBU HAS GONE OUT. BHOLU BEAR MISSING? OKAY, I WILL SEND SHAMBU.

SAVE THE TIGER

IT LOOKED LIKE SHAMBU WOULD NOT HAVE TO GO TOO FAR TO SEARCH FOR BHOLU BEAR.

SOB! I HAVE LOST MY WAY...WISH I HADN'T LEFT HOME.

MASTER IS SURE TO COME LOOKING FOR ME. I WILL HIDE BEHIND THIS TREE TILL THEN.

WATCH OUT, BHOLU BEAR. THAT'S SHIKARI SHAMBU'S BACKYARD!

WHEN SHAMBU RETURNED FROM THE MARKET —

MR RATAN FROM DIAMOND SANCTUARY HAD CALLED. BHOLU BEAR IS MISSING.

LET THEM MISS THE BEAR. I HAVE TO CURE MY INSOMNIA.

SHAMBU GOT TO WORK, PUTTING UP THE HAMMOCK IN THE BACKYARD.

HMM... THAT'S READY. SHANTI, DON'T DISTURB ME.

BANANAS, SLURP!

AAHA... DON'T THINK I NEED A BANANA... ZZZZZZ.

RIPE DELICIOUS BANANAS, HERE I COME!

MEANWHILE —

LET ME GO CHECK IF THE BANANAS WORKED. THEN I CAN ORDER SOME MORE.

DID SHE HAVE A BANANA TOO?

AND IN THE BACKYARD —

THEY ... MUNCH... TASTE A LITTLE STRANGE ...MUNCH.

CHOMP CHOMP

38

SHIKARI SHAMBU

LION LORE

Based on a story sent
by : **V. Vignesh,**

Illustrations :
Savio Mascarenhas

ONE DAY JJ DROPPED IN AT SHAMBU'S HOME.

I'M SOON GOING TO CATCH A LION, SHAMBU.... AND PEOPLE WILL CALL ME THE BRAVE ONE.

ZZZZZZ

I'M TALKING ABOUT YOU. YOU NEVER LISTEN......BLAH! BLAH!

MMPH, SHAMBU HAS ALREADY CAUGHT OVER A HUNDRED THOUSAND LIONS. HAVEN'T YOU, SHAMBU?

HUH? YES.. YES! HE HAS?

JUST THEN —

ATTENTION EVERYONE! A LION FROM THE FOREST RESERVE HAS BEEN SPOTTED ON THE STREETS. AN AWARD OF RS 5000/- TO ANYONE WHO CAN BRING HIM BACK ALIVE.

THAT'S MY LION, STAND OUT OF MY WAY. HERE I COME!

HUMPH!

HE WENT AND SAT NEAR THE MEAT FOR A GOOD LONG TIME.

SNARL...GRRR... ...YAWNNNN...

COME ON, YOU DUMB LION, EAT THE MEAT

SNIFF! SNIFF!

POOF!

COULD THERE BE SOME PROBLEM WITH THE MEAT??

GROWL

AAH!

AND THEN —

AAAAAH!

AFTER A LONG TIME —

IS THIS A NEW KIND OF BAIT?

SHUT UP AND GET ME DOWN, SHAMBU.

OH WELL, OKAY, JJ, HANG ON!

Noooo! Ooooh!

CRASH RUMBLE

JJ, JJ, WAKE UP!

SNORE

HETA

HEY, WHAT'S THAT SOUND FROM THE VAN?

SNNNORE

THE LION! IT'S FAST ASLEEP IN JJ'S VAN.

WELL, I'LL DO JJ A FAVOUR AND DRIVE THE LION BACK TO THE SANCTUARY.

OFF WE GO TO THE FOREST RESERVE! AND SHANTI SAYS I'M THE LAZY ONE! HUH! WAIT TILL I TAKE HER ON THAT VACATION.

HETA

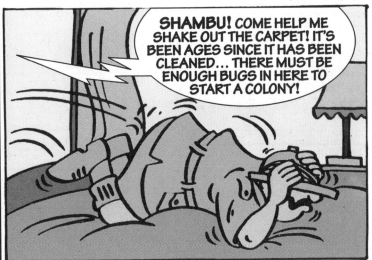

shikari shambu and The shapeshifter

Writer:
Rajani Thindiath

Illustrations:
Savio Mascarenhas

Colouring:
Rajesh Phatak

SHAMBU! COME HELP ME SHAKE OUT THE CARPET! IT'S BEEN AGES SINCE IT HAS BEEN CLEANED... THERE MUST BE ENOUGH BUGS IN HERE TO START A COLONY!

SPRING CLEANING! I HATE THAT WORD! I'M SURE THE BUGS HATE IT TOO! IF SHANTI WOULD JUST LEAVE THEM AND ME ALONE!!

TRRRRRRING! TRRRRRRNNNNG!

HELLO... OH, FOREST OFFICER BAIG! HOW ARE YOU!

I'M IN BIG TROUBLE, SHAMBU! YOU'VE GOT TO HELP ME!!

WHAT'S THE MATTER?

WE WERE SUPPOSED TO START OUR NIGHT SAFARI DAY AFTER TOMORROW BUT OUR FOREST GUIDE HAS QUIT ALL OF A SUDDEN! IF I CAN'T GET A REPLACEMENT I'LL BE IN A SOUP... I WAS WONDERING IF...

YOU WANT ME TO TAKE THE JOB? CERTAINLY, BAIG! ANYTHING TO HELP!

RIGHT ON TIME TO ESCAPE SHANTI'S SPRING CLEANING!

THANK YOU SHAMBU, THANK YOU! I KNEW I COULD RELY ON YOU!

45

GRRRRRROWL!

WH-WHAT'S THAT?

THE T-TIGER!

LOOK! A MAN!

AAAAAAARGH!

IT'S NOT A MAN! IT'S A TIGER!

IT'S THE TIGER-MAN! THE SHAPESHIFTER!

WHAT A HORRIBLE CREATURE! I'D BETTER ESCAPE FROM THE BACK DOOR BEFORE IT BREAKS IN!

GRRRRRROWL!

THERE IT IS AGAIN! MR. SHAMBU DO SOMETHING!... MR. SHAMBU? MR. SHAMBU!

48

LET'S GET OUT OF HERE!

?! ●●●

SHAPESHIFTER!

GET HIM!

UUUFH! AH! OUCH!

THE NEXT DAY, AT MR. BAIG'S OFFICE –

IF IT HAD NOT BEEN FOR THE COURAGE SHOWN BY OUR BRAVE MR. SHAMBU THE RUMOURS OF THE SHAPESHIFTER WOULD'VE TANKED THE NIGHT SAFARI FROM THE WORD GO!

THOSE TWO MEN WERE POACHERS! THEY WERE HELPED BY AN OLD WOMAN. THEY WANTED TO CREATE A SCARE SO VILLAGERS WOULD STAY AT HOME AND NOT BOTHER THEM WHILE THEY WERE POACHING!

TRRRRRR TRRRNNNNG

HELLO... OH, HELLO MRS. SHAMBU... CERTAINLY...

THAT WAS YOUR WIFE, SHAMBU. SHE WANTS YOU HOME.

PUSH IT FURTHER, PUSH IT FURTHER!

IT'S EASIER TO DEAL WITH A SHAPESHIFTER THAN TO SHIFT FURNITURE! OOOOF!

SHIKARI SHAMBU

Precious Catch

This story won a consolation prize in the Shambu story competition

Based on a story sent by : Sarayu Vasan,

Illustrations : **Savio Mascarenhas**

SHAMBU WAS ALL ALONE AT HOME.

YEEPS! THIS IS A SCARY BOOK.

TREMBLE TREMBLE

GHOSTS AND GHOULS

JUST THEN —

KNOCK KNOCK

YAARGH! IT'S THE GILLIGILLI GHOST FROM GOCHIPUR!

NO, IT'S ME, MURTHY. I NEED YOUR HELP.

MR MURTHY WAS A FRIEND.

AFTER THINGS HAD CALMED DOWN A BIT—

SO YOU WANT MY HELP IN GETTING RID OF A BLACK BEAR.

YES, HE COMES AND RUINS MY GARDEN AND TRIES TO GET INTO THE KITCHEN! I AM SCARED.

I AM SCARED TOO, MURTHY. YOU SLEEP HERE TONIGHT AND I'LL COME OVER WITH YOU TOMORROW.

ALL RIGHT.

AND SO THE TWO BRAVE MEN KEPT EACH OTHER COMPANY.

THE NEXT DAY —

WHY DID YOU HAVE TO BUILD A HOUSE IN THE MIDDLE OF A JUNGLE?

I DIDN'T. MY GRANDMOTHER DID.

THIS IS YOUR ROOM. MAKE YOURSELF COMFORTABLE.

WHERE ARE YOU OFF TO?

I'LL GO TO THE VILLAGE AND TELL THE VILLAGERS TO COME AND HELP YOU IN THE HUNT.

AFTER MURTHY HAD GONE, SHAMBU EXPLORED THE HOUSE.

EEP! WHO'S THIS?

SOMETHING FELL OUT OF THE BACK.

IT'S A NOTE WHICH SAYS, 'RAJA'S TREASURE HERE!'

THIS IS CERTAINLY MURTHY'S GRANDMOTHER AND SHE HAS LEFT A SECRET MAP FOR A HIDDEN TREASURE...

...WHAT LUCK!

MURTHY ISN'T HERE BUT NEVER MIND. I'LL HAVE A SURPRISE FOR HIM WHEN HE COMES.

SHIKARI SHAMBU HUNTED AROUND THE HOUSE FOR THE SPOT DESCRIBED IN THE MAP.

FOUR TREES IN A PERFECT SQUARE.. HMM...

...HERE THEY ARE! THAT WAS EASY.

I MUST MARK THE EXACT MIDDLE AND START DIGGING.

SHIKARI SHAMBU DUG...

YECH! A BONE.

...AND DUG...

BLECH! ANOTHER BONE.

...BUT THERE WAS NO TREASURE.

WHEW! THERE'S NOTHING DOWN HERE. I THINK I'LL CLIMB OUT AND REST FOR A WHILE.

BUT JUST AS SHIKARI SHAMBU CAME OUT—

GRRROWL.

YIKES! IT'S THE BLAB..BLOOK.. BLEEK..BLACK.. BLAIR!

YES, IT WAS THE BIG BLACK BEAR AND IT LOOKED VERY VERY BAD TEMPERED.

HOLD IT! I AM UNARMED. I AM HELPLESS.

SNARL

THE BEAR WAS NOT MOVED. IT SPRANG FORWARD...

GRRR...

HELP!

... AND FELL INTO THE FRESHLY-DUG PIT.

UNGH!

A LITTLE LATER —

SHAMBU, YOU GOT THE BEAR SINGLE-HANDED!

THANKS TO YOUR GRANDMOTHER.

AFTER HE HAD READ THE NOTE MURTHY LAUGHED UPROARIOUSLY.

NO WONDER YOU DIDN'T FIND ANY TREASURE. RAJA WAS OUR DOG AND THIS NOTE MUST HAVE BEEN WRITTEN BY MY BROTHER WHEN WE WERE STILL KIDS.

RAJA.. A DOG.. NO WONDER! HEH! HEH!

53

SHIKARI SHAMBU
Shambu's Summer Camp

Based on a story sent by:

Shalini Keshav,

Illustrations:
Savio Mascarenhas

SHIKARI SHAMBU'S NEPHEW, VIVEK, WAS SPENDING HIS SUMMER HOLIDAYS WITH HIM.

UNCLE IS SLEEPING AGAIN.

I KNOW. HE IS TIRED.

WHY? WHAT HAS HE DONE?

ER ... WELL .....

HE KNOWS SO MUCH ABOUT ANIMALS AND FORESTS. WHY CAN'T HE HOLD A SUMMER CAMP FOR MY FRIENDS AND ME?

SUMMER CAMP ... HMM ... NOT A BAD IDEA.

AND SO —

TAKE CARE OF VIVEK AND HIS FRIENDS. HAVE A GOOD TIME, BOYS.

HOW DID THIS HAPPEN!?

WE WILL, AUNTY SHANTI!

THEY HAD A GREAT TIME.

THAT IS THE WOODPECKER. HIS NEST IS IN THE HOLE IN THE TREE.

TAP TAP TAP

IT IS ...

...OUCH ! ...

... BETTER TO LEAVE IT ALONE.

TAP

CAN WE PLUCK SOME OF THESE GUAVAS FOR DINNER? THEY ARE RIPE.

ALL RIGHT.

DID YOU HAVE TO PLUCK SO MANY?

I'LL KEEP SOME OF THEM FOR TOMORROW, UNCLE SHAMBU.

KEEP THEM IN MY TENT. IF YOU EAT TOO MANY YOU'LL GET A TUMMY ACHE.

DASH IT! I THOUGHT WE'D HAVE A MIDNIGHT FEAST.

THE MOON ROSE HIGH IN THE SKY AS NIGHT FELL GENTLY ON THE FOREST. IN A DEEP CAVE NEAR BY A GREY FORM STIRRED.

HUNGRY ... I AM HUNGRY.

IT WAS A HUGE SLOTH BEAR.

THE GREAT BEAR AMBLED OUT AND SNIFFED THE AIR.

SNIFF

SNIFF

IT COULD SMELL SOMETHING!

GRUNT ... SLURP ... SNIFF ... YUM!

OH NO! IT WAS HEADING STRAIGHT FOR THE CAMP.

FOOD! JUICY FOOD!

AARGH! IT WAS MAKING STRAIGHT FOR SHIKARI SHAMBU'S TENT.

IS THIS THE END OF OUR BRAVE SHIKARI?

NO! IT WAS THE END OF THE GUAVAS.

SNIFF

SLURP YUM

AND THEN A STRONG ARM SHOT OUT.

STEALING THE GUAVAS, EH!? YOU BOYS THOUGHT YOU COULD FOOL ME.

CRUNCH

MUNCH

THE STARTLED SLOTH BEAR SHOVED SHIKARI SHAMBU AND SCURRIED OUT.

WAIT HERE, YOU LITTLE IMP!

THE SLOTH BEAR PURSUED BY A CAP-BLINDED SHAMBU SPED INTO THE FOREST.

UNCLE SHAMBU!

COME HERE, YOU BRAT!

BUT THEY DID NOT GO FAR.

GRUNT! OH NO! A TRAP!

THE POOR OLD SLOTH BEAR HAD FALLEN INTO A POACHER'S TRAP.

UH ... HUH ... THE CHILD HAS FALLEN INTO A PIT. WHAT WILL HIS PARENTS SAY? I HAD BETTER GO AND GET HELP.

HELP HAD ALREADY ARRIVED. VIVEK HAD CALLED AUNT SHANTI AND SHE HAD ALERTED THE FOREST OFFICIALS.

MR SHAMBU, IS THERE A PROBLEM?

ER ... YES .. ER... THAT WAY.

WHEN THEY REACHED THE PIT

YOU CHASED A SLOTH BEAR! AND YOU HAVE HELPED US EXPOSE A POACHER'S TRAP! YOU ARE A HERO!

I DID? I HAVE? I AM?

THE REST OF THE CAMP WAS QUITE A SUCCESS.

FISHING ALLOWED FOR BIRDS ONLY

AND THAT IS A KINGFISHER ... BLAH ... BLAH....

YES, UNCLE SHAMBU.

OF COURSE, UNCLE SHAMBU.

THE BOYS WERE IN AWE OF THE GREAT SHIKARI.

SHIKARI SHAMBU

SKIING WITH WOLVES

Reader's Choice

Based on a story sent by:
Bhushan B. Poojary,

Illustrations: Savio Mascarenhas

SHAMBU AND SHANTI HAD BEEN INVITED TO KASHMIR FOR A WILDLIFE CONVENTION.

BRR..RR..IT WILL BE FREEZING COLD.

LET'S GO. IT WILL BE FUN TO PLAY IN THE SNOW.

SHANTI HAD HER WAY.

HUFF.. PUFF!

AND SOON THEY WERE OFF.

IN KASHMIR — WHAT A PLEASURE IT IS TO HAVE A GREAT HUNTER LIKE YOU AMIDST US!

HE ALWAYS HOGS ALL THE LIMELIGHT. THIS TIME I'LL GET HIM.

IT WAS SHAMBU'S RIVAL, J.J.

THE NEXT DAY — LET'S GO PLAY IN THE SNOW, SHAMBU.

I AM GOING SKIING.

SHAMBUJI, YOU HAVE TO HELP US.

SURE.. SURE.. I WILL.

FOUR WOLVES HAVE BEEN ENTERING OUR HOUSES AND EATING OUR FOOD.

WOLVES! GULP!

WOLVES! THIS IS MY CHANCE. YES!

SURE, SHAMBU WILL HELP. HE ALWAYS HELPS. BEST OF LUCK, SHAMBU.

THANK YOU, SHAMBUJI.

PAT PAT

HOW DID I GET CAUGHT IN THIS? BUT LET ME GO SKIING FIRST.

HEE! HEE! I HAVE STUCK A PIECE OF PAPER, THAT SMELLS OF MEAT, BEHIND SHAMBU. NOW, I SHALL SEE.

AND SOON—

WHAT A HEAVENLY SMELL OF MEAT.

TIME TO GO BACK AND EAT.

GRUMBLE GRUMBLE

ULP! WOLVES! RUN..NO, NO.. SKI!

NOT FAR AWAY —

SNIFF SNIFF

WHAT A BONUS! MONEY, JEWELLERY PLUS ALL THIS YUMMY FOOD.

SOB

SNIFF

TWO GUN-TOTING DACOITS HAD JUST LOOTED A BUS.

BUT —

CRASH

SLURP!

WHERE'S THE BAG OF JEWELLERY?

GAK!

STOP!

EEE..YAAH...

...AAAH....

FASTER! HE SHOULDN'T ESCAPE.

60

GULP! I AM HEADING STRAIGHT FOR THE FIR TREE. I'LL CRASH INTO IT.

JUST THEN —

SPLAT

IT WAS SHANTI.

HA! HA! GOT HIM! I SHOULD QUICKLY GO BEFORE SHAMBU NOTICES.

BUT...

THUD! THUD! THUD! THUD! THUD!

...THE OTHERS WERE NOT SO LUCKY.

TWEET

SOON —

THE STATE HAS AWARDED RS 40,000 FOR CATCHING THESE DACOITS.

I'LL LEAVE THESE WOLVES FAR AWAY IN THE FOREST.

HOW DID YOU DO IT, SHAMBUJI?

OH! IT WAS A SNOWBALL THAT SAVED THE DAY. HA! HA!

HMPH!

SHIKARI SHAMBU

THE FOREST YETI

This story won a Consolation Prize in the Shikari Shambu Story-writing Competition.

Based on a story
sent by : Sasi S. Nagarajan,

Illustrations :
Savio Mascarenhas

THE VILLAGERS OF DALEGAON HAD A PEACEFUL AND HAPPY WAY OF LIFE.

AH! LOOK AT MY HUGE HAUL OF HERBS.

I'VE GOT A GOOD COLLECTION OF FIREWOOD TOO.

THEIR VILLAGE WAS AT THE EDGE OF A LUSH GREEN FOREST CALLED, HARAGIRI.

THIS WEEK WE WILL MAKE SOME GOOD MONEY AT THE TOWN MARKET.

YES! NOWADAYS OUR HERBS FETCH A GOOD PRICE.

OUR FOREST HARAGIRI IS A GENEROUS BENEFACTOR.

WE MUST DEDICATE OUR FEAST TO THE FOREST AS USUAL.

IN THIS HAVEN OF PEACE THERE WAS SOON A HINT OF TROUBLE.

OHH! HELP! HELP!!

WHAT HAPPENED?

M-M-MONSTER! THERE IS A MONSTER IN THE FOREST!

OH DEAR! YOU ALWAYS WERE AN IMAGINATIVE CHILD.

BUT —

THERE IS SOMETHING WEIRD IN THERE.

SOMETHING BLACK AND HUGE AND HAIRY!

THE FEAR OF THE FIERCE CREATURE FORCED THE VILLAGERS TO KEEP OUT OF THE FOREST.

WE CAN'T GO ON LIKE THIS. WE'LL STARVE.

LET'S CALL THE CONSTABLE FROM THE TOWN TO HELP US.

THE CONSTABLE WAS DISTURBED BY THE DESCRIPTION OF THE CREATURE.

THIS CALLS FOR AN EXPERT'S OPINION — THE ONE AND ONLY SHIKARI SHAMBU.

OH! DO CALL HIM!

SO IT WAS THAT TWO DAYS LATER SHIKARI SHAMBU LED THE CONSTABLE AND A FEW OF THE VILLAGERS INTO THE FOREST OF HARAGIRI.

THUMP

THUMP

WHAT'S THAT?

A LAND-SLIDE?

NO! SOMEONE IS THROWING ROCKS AT US.

I CAN SEE IT! A BIG BLACK HAIRY CREATURE.

THE CREATURE JUMPED DOWN TO A LOWER BRANCH.

IT HAS HORNS!

SUCH LONG CLAWS.

BUT IT'S UPRIGHT LIKE AN APE.

THE CREATURE BEGAN TO GROWL AS IT PELTED CLODS OF MUD ON THE MEN.

GRRR

I THINK WE'D BETTER GO.

BEFORE HE COULD COMPLETE HIS SENTENCE, ALL THE OTHERS HAD BEGUN TO RUN...

OUCH!

EEKS!

AHH!

...ALL EXCEPT SHIKARI SHAMBU.

THEY RETURNED TO THE VILLAGE, BATTERED, BRUISED AND TERRIFIED.

SO SCARY! THE ROAR, THE CLAWS....

WHAT COULD IT BE?

MEANWHILE SHIKARI SHAMBU WAS PUZZLING OVER THE SAME THOUGHT.

IN THE SNOWCLAD MOUNTAINS, I'D ONCE CHASED THE ABOMINABLE SNOWMAN OR YETI.

COULD THIS BE A COUNTRY COUSIN? A FOREST YETI?

AFTER A WHILE, SHIKARI SHAMBU CLAMBERED OUT OF HIS HIDING PLACE.

WHERE ARE THE OTHERS?

HE TRIED TO FIND HIS WAY BACK TO THE VILLAGE.

OH! ALL THE TREES LOOK THE SAME, IT'S GETTING DARK TOO!

AT DUSK, THERE WERE THE USUAL JUNGLE NOISES.

WOO-OOO-OOO

YIKES! SOMETHING IS SNAPPING AT MY LEGS!

CLUK!

CLUK!!

HE QUICKLY CLAMBERED UP THE NEAREST TREE, COVERED THICKLY WITH VINES.

AH! THIS IS AS GOOD A PLACE AS ANY TO SPEND THE NIGHT.

OR SO HE THOUGHT. JUST THEN —

CRACK

YOW!

THE BRANCH SNAPPED UNDER HIS WEIGHT AND DOWN HE FELL...

...TILL HIS FALL WAS SUDDENLY BROKEN.

OUF! WHERE AM I?

IT WAS ON SOFT THICK HAY THAT HE HAD LANDED.

WHEN HE HAD STOPPED FEELING DIZZY —

IT IS A HUT! THERE'S LIGHT INSIDE. WHO COULD BE LIVING HERE?

THERE WERE PILES OF DRYING HERBS, HONEYCOMBS DRENCHED WITH HONEY, AND LOGS, NEATLY SAWED AND SIZED, LAID OUT ON THE FLOOR OF THE HUT.

OH! I CAN'T BELIEVE THIS. HERE COMES THE CREATURE!

THE BLACK, HAIRY, HORNED CREATURE REMOVED HIS HORNS, HIS CLAWS AND EVEN HIS FUR.

WHY! IT'S A MAN, WHAT A TRICK!!

SHIKARI SHAMBU FELT IT WAS HIS DUTY TO NAB THE CREATURE.

I MUST SCARE HIM BY SHOOTING IN THE AIR. WHERE'S MY GUN?

AS USUAL, HE FUMBLED...

...AND INSTEAD OF HIS GUN, HE PULLED A BAMBOO SUPPORTING THE ROOF.

THE NEXT MINUTE —

PLONK!

THUD

HE FELL RIGHT ON TOP OF HIS VICTIM, KNOCKING HIM DOWN.

IS HE DEAD? NO, I'M NOT SO HEAVY. ANYWAY LET ME TIE HIM UP TO BE ON THE SAFE SIDE.

DEALING WITH UNCONSCIOUS MEN OR BEASTS BROUGHT OUT THE BRAVEST TRAITS OF OUR SHIKARI!

TRA LA LA!

MEANWHILE AT THE VILLAGE —

SHIKARI SHAMBU HASN'T RETURNED.

WE MUST SEARCH FOR HIM. HE IS OUR GUEST.

BUT IT'S SO SCARY IN THE FOREST.

WE'LL TAKE SHIKARI SHAMBU'S JEEP. THE LIGHTS WILL SCARE THE CREATURE AND WE CAN ALSO ESCAPE EASILY.

SOON —

WHAT'S THAT? SOUNDS LIKE MY JEEP.

SHAMBUJI! WHERE ARE YOU?

SOON —

HERE! I'VE GOT YOUR WILD CREATURE ALL BOUND AND READY FOR YOU.

OH! YOU ARE A BRAVE MAN INDEED.

THIS IS GOTIA! HE EXPORTS FOREST PRODUCE.

HE MUST BE USING THIS DISGUISE TO SCARE OUR PEOPLE.

BUT HE WAS NO MATCH FOR OUR BRAVE SHIKARI SHAMBU.

ARMED WITH A REWARD AND A RICH HAUL OF FOREST PRODUCE, SHIKARI SHAMBU RETURNED HOME TRIUMPHANT.

I'M HOME WITH HONEY!

BAH! DON'T YOU HONEY ME! YOU'VE BEEN WATCHING TOO MUCH T.V.

NO! REAL GENUINE HONEY FROM THE FOREST.

Shikari Shambu
Night of the Bats

Writer:
Rajani Thindiath
Illustrations:
Savio Mascarenhas
Colouring:
Rajesh Phatak

OOOOF! WHAT A SMELL!

NOW I REMEMBER WHAT HE SAID HE WAS GROWING!

DURIAN! WORLD'S SMELLIEST FRUIT!

NO WONDER THE ORCHARD WAS NOT A SUCCESS!

I MUST TELL SHANTI I FOUND IT.

DRAT! NO NETWORK!

I'D BETTER START BACK FOR THE HOTEL! BUT I'LL TAKE THAT DURIAN TO SHOW SHANTI.

COULDN'T EXPECT ANYTHING BETTER FROM RAGHU, I SUPPOSE. I'LL HAVE TO THINK OF WHAT TO DO WITH THAT ORCHARD.

SHAMBU HAD WORKED UP A GREAT THIRST AND HE WAS LOOKING FORWARD TO A COLD GLASS OF LASSI AT THE NEAREST VILLAGE. BUT WHEN HE GOT THERE –

ALL THE SHOPS ARE CLOSED, AND IT'S NOT EVEN SIX!

72